The GIANT

and the

mouse

by
Diane Stelling

illustrated by
Luke, Jonathan, and Thomas Stelling

Published by: Hereami Publishing, P.O. Box 261, Butler, NJ 07405-0261; (201) 838-2685; Fax: (201) 492-1525.

Library of Congress Catalog Card Number: 96-95010

ISBN 0-9655758-8-8

Printed by The Print Center, NY, NY, USA

This book is dedicated to my brother Mickey

Dearest Luke, Jon, and Tom,

These poems are for, by, and about the three of you. Without you and your wonderful views of life, I never would have been inspired to write anything.

I want you to learn to laugh at yourselves, at life, and the silly situations we find ourselves in.

I want you to see the farce, beauty, and power of the English language. You can make fun of it, but learn it, for throughout life it will be one of the most powerful tools you have, and no one can take it away from you.

And finally, I want you to know that I *understand*. If only for a brief time, this giant tried to squeeze through the mousehole.

All my love,

Mom

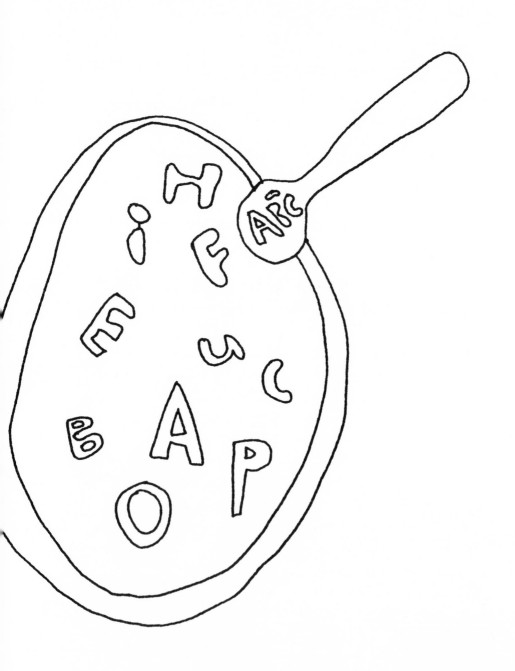

ALPHABET SOUP

Why is *why* spelled w-h-y?
Why isn't *why* spelled **y**?
And why is *eye* spelled e-y-e?
It would make much more sense as **i**.
And who'd think that *you* is spelled y-o-u,
When it seems like **u** is the best,
And why is *see* spelled s-e-e?
When just **c** could get rid of the rest.
My good friend *Jay* is spelled J-a-y,
But it seems that **J** would suffice,
And who thought to spell *are* a-r-e?
When plain **r** seems awfully nice.
And why must *be* be spelled b-e?
The **b** just says it all,
And *gee*, that's another, spelled g-e-e,
The lone **g** would make it small.
If you really like *tea*, why's it t-e-a?
When the **t** is all that's heard,
And the vegetable *pea* is p-e-a,
But **p** alone completes the word.
Oh, the last one is *oh*, and it's spelled o-h,
Although **o** can do it with ease,
So when you're all finished,
    just put it together,
And read these sentences, please:

> **O g, J, u** *can* **c** *with your* **i**
> *There* **r p**s *in your* **t**
> *How can it* **b**?
> *And* **y**?

PUNCTUATION

Period. End of sentence.
They say it all the time.
A question mark asks a question,
What a funny, squiggly line.

Commas here and there,
Like footprints 'tween my words,
Apostrophe marks above the rest,
Like commas made by birds.

When someone's talking on your page,
Quotation marks fly around,
And capture the words and keep them safe,
Without making a sound.

Parentheses are funny things,
They curve and come in twos,
And when they are all stiff and square,
They're brackets, if you choose.

I've heard some talk of colons,
And semi-ones that seem to fly,
It sounds quite serious to me,
Periods and commas piled up high.

I like the dash, it seems so bold,
So sturdy without a joint,
But my favoritest punctuation mark
Is the exclamation point !!!!!!!!!!!!!

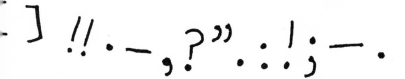

NO MATTER WHAT I SAY
I'M ALWAYS WRONG

I'm gooder at this
Than I thought I would be,
And it's funner than ever
To speak properly.

I sitted in my seat
When I went to school,
And writed in my book
These grammar rules.

Then I slided into base
When I went out to play,
And catched the ball
To save the day.

These rules are so silly
You can see my plight,
Just like I told my Mom
Yesternight!

I JUST FORGOT

Forgot my spelling book,
My milk money,
Vocabulary too,
My homework and permission slip,
What ever should I do?

Forgot my dittos
And my math book,
My sneakers just for gym,
My library book and lunch box,
What terrible trouble I'm in.

I try so hard,
I really do,
To know just what I did,
And remember what to do tomorrow,
I'm only just a kid.

My teacher asks,
And so does Mom,
They put me on the spot,
It seems like all I ever say is -
I just forgot.

WHY
IS SPELLING SO HARD?

Who made up the rules,
About how we should spell?
They just messed it all up,
No, they didn't do well.

Some words sound the same,
But just look at the letters,
They're all twisted around,
And it doesn't get better.

Don't **know** how to spell **no**,
Thought I **knew**, but it's **new**,
Better **not** misspell **knot**,
Blew my nose 'til it's **blue**.

Can't get **peace** when a **piece**
That I **write** isn't **right**,
About **which witch** is **which**,
And which **knight's** out this **night**.

What I **need** when I **knead**,
Is some **flour**, not **flower**,
How 'bout **pairs** of nice **pears**,
For **our** meal in an **hour**?

Also **here's** what I **hear**,
That a **bear** isn't **bare**,
Some **deer** are so **dear**,
And a **hare** has no **hair**.

The worst three aren't **two**,
They're **too** hard **to** be seen,
They're **two**, **too**, and **to**,
You see what I mean?

I'll keep trying my hardest,
But to you I'll confess,
The rules are confusing,
My spelling's a mess!

MY PENMANSHIP IS SUNK

Fat ones, skinny ones,
Standing in a row,
Curved ones, straight ones,
Some are high and some are low.

Above the line, below the line,
Start them in the middle,
Dots are floating in the air,
It seems like quite a riddle.

My teacher's words look crisp and neat,
Like soldiers who are ready,
My letters wander all around,
So jumbled and unsteady.

The leaders of the sentence,
Should be bigger than the rest,
I hope my capitals will grow,
And turn out for the best.

An *h* must try to stand quite tall,
As I stretch its long, long head,
For if I tire and it is short,
An *n* will show instead.

Now *t* presents a problem,
For it's neither short nor tall,
It's somewhere in the middle,
I've no hope for it at all.

My *w*, it needs some work,
For when I leave a space,
I wind up with what seems to be,
Two *v*s looking face-to-face.

The *e* and *s* have minds of their own,
And sometimes seem quite drunk,
With *e* floating way above the line,
And *s* down below - it's sunk.

And then I have to worry if
The letters are all straight,
And if the space between the words
Is way too small or great.

To please my teacher and I dare think
The only way to suit her,
Would be if I could type my work
At home on our computer!

I'VE GOT THE
GHOSH-DARN GH BLUES

Blight, bright, fight,
Flight, fright, knight,
Light, might, night,
Right, plight, sight.
> **The g is silent. Seems easy to me.**

Ghost and ghoul.
> **Hmmm. Well, maybe the h is silent.**

Caught, taught,
High, sigh,
Bought, brought, thought.
> **Nope. The g is silent. I was right.**

Cough, trough,
Rough, tough.
> **Uh-oh. Now the gh sounds like an f.**

Though and bough.
> **Yecch. Is the gh an o or a w?**

That's it.
I'm *thru*.
I've had *enuf*.

TIME'S A-WASTIN'

Hurry up.
You'll miss your bus.
Books away.
Quick, no fuss.

Let's get going.
Finish lunch.
Quickly line up,
Not in a bunch!

Time's up.
Pencils down.
Pass the papers,
Don't look around.

Next ditto.
Lots to do.
Concentrate.
We've got to get through.

Rush, rush, rush, rush, rush, rush, rush -

WHY?

DITTO DITTY

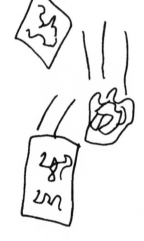

Dittos here,
And dittos there,
Dittos, dittos
Everywhere.

They're on my desk,
And on the floor,
I cannot take it
Anymore.

Table, bed,
Toy airplane wing,
Dittos are on
Everything.

Some are done,
And some are not,
Then there are some that
I forgot.

It's sad to think,
At least one tree,
Has given up its life
For me.

The only way
I'll smile for sure,
Is when all dittos exist
No more.

CHAMELEON

I must be a chameleon.
It seems like
I always try to be like
The people I'm with.
Polite with grownups.
Attentive in school.
Goofy with friends.
Respectful in church.
When am I myself?
Perhaps when I'm alone.
No one to impress.
No one to please.
No one to show off to.
How will anyone
Ever know
The real me?

Do I want them to?

And will I ever really know
Anyone else?

IT'S A SNAP

Press your thumb on middleman,
Push off with all your might,
Then land it on your pointer,
Now practice it, all right?

LOOKS CAN BE DECEIVING

I get confused by all these words
That sound like they have one name,
But when you go to write them down,
They aren't spelled the same.

But the worst ones are, by far I think
These other words I've found,
They look the same on paper,
But have quite a different sound.

I **tear** a paper into bits,
And shed a **tear** for you,
I **read** a nice poem yesterday,
Now, you **read** this one, too.

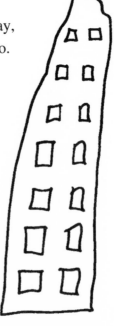

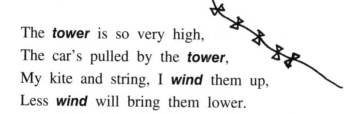

The **tower** is so very high,
The car's pulled by the **tower**,
My kite and string, I **wind** them up,
Less **wind** will bring them lower.

The metal **lead** weighs quite a lot,
I **lead** this group so fine,
I must **present** this nice award,
This **present**, it's all mine.

I'm **live** and hope to get through school,
And **live** so very long,
I **use** these words, but what's the **use**?
They look so nice, but sound all wrong.

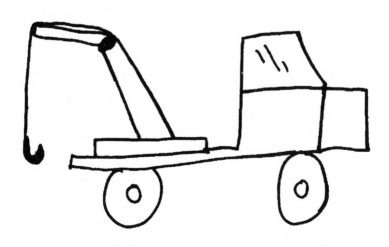

IGNORANT

Dumb.

Stupid.

Idiot.

Jerk.

Those are bad words. Everyone knows that.

Illiterate.

Uneducated.

Impenetrable.

Uninformed.

Big words. They don't sound too bad.

Inane.

Imbecile.

Obtuse.

Illogical.

Wow. Maybe I can be one of those.

HOMEFUN

Homework has always
Bothered me,
It's long and tedious,
Sheer drudgery.

I think it's the name
That makes me run,
Why don't they call it
Homefun?

Work sounds so hard,
I don't want to begin,
But fun is just that,
I'd love to dig in.

So, teachers, if you
Don't want to hear groans,
Give all your students
Some fun to take home!

IT MAKES SENSE TO ME

I just don't seem to get it,
Tho' I've tried so hard and long,
Will someone please just tell me,
Where I've managed to go wrong:

One house, many houses.
One blouse, many blouses.
    Then....one mouse, many mouses.
One box, many boxes.
One fox, many foxes.
    Then....one ox, many oxes.
One noose, many nooses.
One caboose, many cabooses.
    Then....one goose, many gooses.
One leaf, many leaves.
One thief, many thieves.
    Then....one chief, many chieves.

One creep, many creeps.

One peep, many peeps.

    Then....one sheep, many sheeps.

One cheer, many cheers.

One career, many careers.

    Then....one deer, many deers.

One boot, many boots.

One toot, many toots.

    Then....one foot, many foots.

One octopus, many octopi (or octopuses).

One fungus, many fungi (or funguses).

    Then....one asparagus, many asparagi
    (or asparaguses).

I follow all the rules, I do,
I hope my teacher sees,
And 'til someone explains why not,
I'll stick to my *believes!*

PENCIL EATER

I like to sharpen pencils,
And make a fine point at the end,
Then, oops, the tip will break right off,
And I start all over again.

Sometimes the point gets crooked,
One side is wood to the end,
The other side has too much lead,
I keep on going, then.

The wheels keep spinning and grinding,
I really am quite deft,
But by the time I'm finished,
I have no pencil left.

AN INSPIRING THOUGHT

What's inspiration?
It's the spark
That ignites the fire
Within you.

SEEN, BUT NOT HEARD

They call them silent letters,
For they don't make any sound,
And when you aren't looking,
They pop up all around.

Like:

The *hymn* and *psalm* that are sung at church,
The *gnome* out in the wood,
The *sign* that's in the window,
The *bread* that tastes so good.

I *knew* that I was *right*,
You *thought* that I was *wrong*,
I *know* that I can *write* this *right*,
And not be *wrong* for long.

They're in some very short words,
Like the ever-popular *gnu*,
And in some very long words,
Like *psychiatrist* and *pterodactyl*, too.

Shhh!!

There's something wrong, it bothers me,
Although they do persist,
It's like they have no meaning,
Why, then, do they exist?

They're quiet and ignored and yet,
When people go to write,
They get upset at silent letters,
They're in the way, all right.

Why is this such a bother?
Why should I even care?
Because of something adults say,
A feeling I don't share.

They tell me kids are noisy,
They shouldn't say a word,
And just like these poor letters,
They should be seen, but not heard.

MANNERS

If I were a Mom
I wouldn't be
A nervous wreck
About me.

I'll grow up
I know all this stuff,
Why does she make
My life so rough?

Don't jump on the couch,
Move away from the TV,
Feet off the table,
Sit properly.

Don't talk with your mouth,
Stuffed full of food,
Use a napkin,
Tie your shoes.

Quit making faces,
Always say please,
Talk with respect,
Cover your sneeze.

It's all boring,
Can't she see?
None of it
Applies to me.

If I wanted to
I'd do it all,
But just for now,
I'm havin' a ball!

When I grow up,
And have kids of my own,
I won't ever bug 'em,
I'll leave 'em alone.

THE GIANT AND THE MOUSE

They don't understand,
Never have, never will,
Even when I'm grown up,
It'll puzzle me still.

They don't take the time,
To listen at all,
My ideas have no value,
Perhaps I'm too small.

I know of their world,
Big thoughts, work, and money,
Always rushing around,
No time to be funny.

They don't know my world,
Can't fit in, always wrong,
So when I'm with them,
I just tag along.

I don't understand
What's wrong, is it me?
They ignore all my feelings,
Why can't they see?

The mouse can fit through the giant's door,
But the giant can't fit through the mouse's.

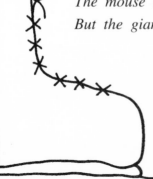

HOW DO YOU MAKE....?

How do you make ketchup?
    Squeeze a tomato, that's how.
How do you make orange juice?
    Squeeze an orange, that's how.
How do you make peanut butter?
    Squeeze a peanut, that's how.
How do you make milk?
    Squeeze a cow, that's how.
How do you make jelly?
    Squeeze a berry, that's how.
How do you make an egg?
    Squeeze a chicken, that's how.
How do you make a kiss?
    Squeeze your lips, that's how.
How do you make a hug?
    Squeeze your kids, oh wow!

WHY ME?

What did I do?
I don't see.
I forgot the question.
Don't call on me.

What do you mean?
I don't understand.
I didn't do it.
Why'd I raise my hand?

What's the assignment?
I'm not done.
I don't have the answer.
Which one?

I'm always confused,
You can plainly see,
Why does it only
Happen to me?

MR. MOON

Hi, Mr. Moon,
Glad to see you tonight,
This world really needs,
A gigantic night light.

It's dark and it's scary,
When you aren't here,
I wait and I wonder,
Will you ever appear?

But you always return,
Like a big sideways smile,
So, goodnight, Mr. Moon,
Stick around for awhile.

LIFE OR DEATH?

Why do things have to die?
It just isn't fair.

No one likes to talk about death.
It must be scary.

When you die, it's over.
No life, laughter, fun.

There's nothing.

But I remember things that have died.
Flowers, my cat, Grandma.

I remember how they looked.
How pretty they were.

I remember what we did together.
The fun we had.

I remember how I loved them.
And how they loved me.

Maybe when things die,
They're still here.

Just quieter, gentler.
In our minds, our hearts.

But always here.

If this is death, then I wonder -
What will people remember about me?

THAT'S WHAT BROTHERS
AND SISTERS ARE FOR

To make fun of
To pick on
To rat on
And tease.
To fight with
To make cry
To hit
If you please.
To be nasty
To hide from
To pinch
And to bite.
To be mean
To pull hair
To kick
Out of sight.
To play games
To ride bikes
To pretend
And have fun.
To tell jokes
To be near
To protect
From everyone.

WHAT'D I DO WRONG?

Time out.
Go to your room.
No TV, no cartoons.
Think about it.
Apologize.
Smarten up and get wise.

It's not fair!
It wasn't **my** fault.

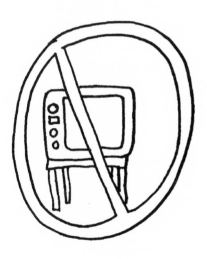

MAGINATION

Everyone's got one.
It's a pretty powerful thing.
The key to the universe -
And it's free.

When things get boring,
I take out my magination,
Dust it off,
I'm ready to go.

My magination takes me places
Where nothing is bad.
I'm a hero.
Life is wonderful.

My magination brings me friends.
We don't fight, usually,
But if we do,
I win.

I can even go back through time,
And change things that hurt,
That were wrong.
With my magination.

What a wonderful thing!
When life's too much or not enough,
I can escape.
Yup, just me and my magination.

WHAT'S IN A NAME?

Animals come in different groups,
That have such funny names,
Whoever thought the darn words up,
Was certainly playing games.

We know that sheep come in a **flock**,
And buffaloes in a **herd**,
While lions travel in a **pride**,
This is all quite absurd.

Now baby chicks come in a **brood**,
And bees are in a **swarm**,
Geese all gather in a **gaggle**,
Would one word do any harm?

Wolves roam all around in a **pack**,
And fish swim in a **school**,
Ants work together in an **army**,
Too many words, too many rules.

Each animal group has a different name,
But people are, by far,
The group that has the greatest words,
To tell just what they are:

A **bunch**, a **horde**, a **drove**, a **crowd**,
A **congregation**, too,
A **gang**, a **mob**, a **troop**, **assembly**,
These are just a few.

So what does all this mean to us?
I guess, well, nothing, really,
We make such a fuss describing ourselves,
It's all so very silly!

DOODLE BUG

Oh doodle bug, oh doodle bug,
Wherever have you been?
My paper looks so empty,
I just need you back again.

This talk is very boring,
Can't listen anymore,
Let's decorate this paper now,
Before I start to snore.

Let's fill up all the circles
On my letters, if you please,
Then draw a squiggle 'round the page,
You do it all with ease.

We can make a pretty flower,
Or a monster if you like,
A house with trees and children,
Or the fastest racing bike.

This looks so neat, it really does,
We two can be quite proud,
But doodle bug, I wonder,
Why's the talking getting loud?

What?   Huh?   Who me?   The answer?....

MOMMIES DON'T KNOW EVERYTHING

She has eyes in the back of her head, she says,
But I know that isn't true,
She can't always see what I do wrong,
She doesn't have a clue.

And worse than that, she blames me for
Some things I've never done,
It's the other kids, I always say,
But with her I've never won.

Yet, one thing I am sure about,
When my side she doesn't see,
If I convince her she is wrong,
She'll apologize to me.

I'M SCARED....

Of bogeymen,
Of stormy nights,
Of crashing thunder,
No night light.

Of hooting owls,
Of biting things,
Of creepy-crawlies,
Bats with wings.

Of howling wolves,
Of bugs and snakes,
Of ugly monsters,
Big earthquakes.

BOOM!

Of doctor's shots,
Of bad nightmares,
Of getting hurt,
No one cares.

Of being alone,
Of failing tests,
Of having no friends,
Not being the best.

Why'm I scared?
I don't know -
I'm even scared
Of my shadow!

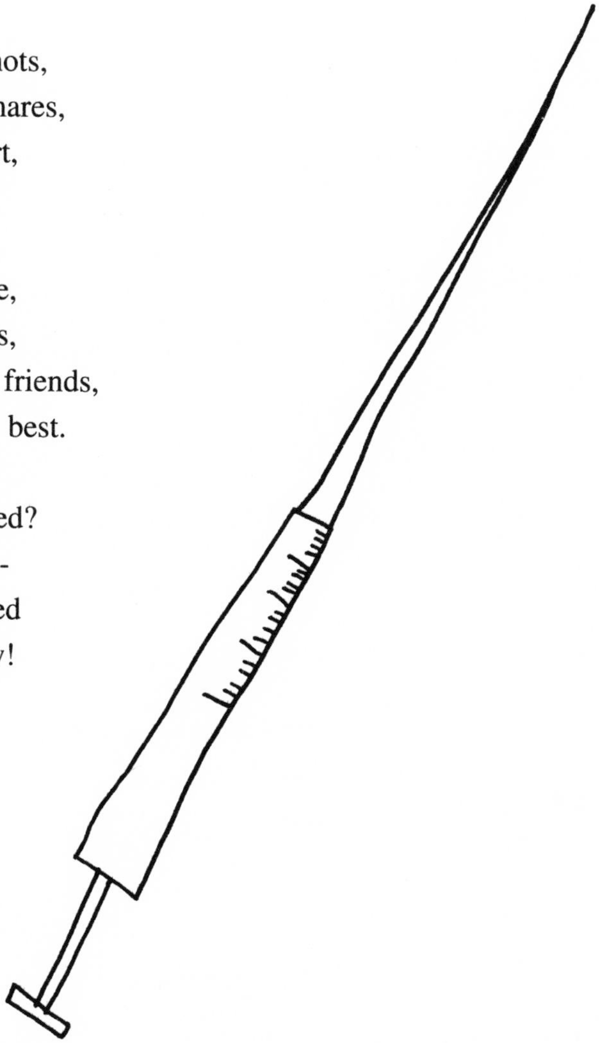

THE TELEPHONE

Please don't ring, oh please don't ring,
I won't know what to do,
I'll pick it up and blurt right out
" Hello....who are **you**? "

I know that's wrong, my Mom said so,
I must be quite polite,
But I won't remember what to say,
If the phone should ring tonight.

I'll say my name and ask them theirs,
And listen like a mouse,
But what will happen if that voice
Has dialed the wrong house?

Or worse than that, the thing I dread,
Because my Mom's not here,
Is if they want to leave a message,
I'll just hang up, I fear.

It's bad, I know, but there's one more thing,
That is the worst of all,
It's when I want to talk to a friend,
And have to **make** a call.

I pick the phone up and dial away,
And hope that I don't miss,
And when they answer I loudly say
" Hello....who is *this*? "

That's wrong, that's wrong, I know that's wrong,
It makes me want to groan,
My manners seem to leave my head,
When I talk into the phone.

I can do it, I know I can,
But one thing makes me scream,
It's when I call somebody's house,
And get their answering machine!

TWO-WHEELER

I can't do this,
I'm too dumb,
I'll learn to ride
When I'm eighty-one.
What was wrong
With my training wheels?
They took 'em away,
Don't care how I feel.
How can you start
Straight up in mid-air?
I'll never do it.
I don't care.
How can you stop?
Where is the brake?
You put down your feet,
What a mistake.
How can you turn
To the left or right,
When you're going as fast as
The speed of light?
You wobble and fall,
And scrape you knees,
Don't like this bike,
Gimme a scooter, please!

LOSING MY FIRST TOOTH

I've had them all my life...........almost.
It's ready to come out...............almost.
I'm pretty happy about it...........almost.
But what if there's none to replace it?

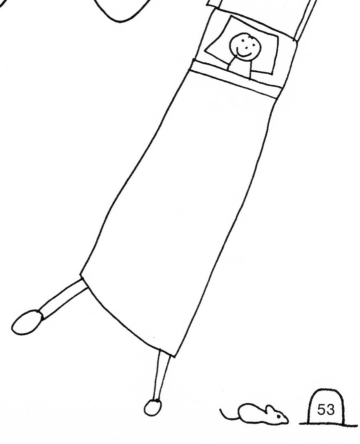

53

MY BEST FRIEND

I can tell her anything.
She never gets tired.
We never fight.

She's always been with me.
Always protects me.
Talks to me.

She never doubts me.
Never gets afraid.
I love her.

She's very pretty.
She likes kisses
And is cuddly.

She does whatever she wants.
Her Mom doesn't yell at her.
She never has tantrums.

There's just one thing
About my best friend
I don't like.

When we take baths,
I go into the tub,
But she doesn't.

My Mom says
She has to go
Into the washer and dryer.

REAL MAGIC

I know that Santa lives all year,
In a place called the cold North Pole,
He makes his toys and feeds his deer,
And at Christmas he's ready to roll.

But what about the Easter Bunny?
I wonder where's **it's** den?
And why's **it** bring pretty eggs to us?
Why not an Easter hen?

Jack Frost, I know, comes when it's cold,
And on the panes puts ice,
But what is he and where's he live,
When it's spring and the weather is nice?

The sandman fills my eyes at night,
But the light must be too dim,
Where does he get the sand he uses?
I'd like to talk to him.

The tooth fairy is the best of all,
She leaves me lots of money,
But what does she need with all the teeth?
I find that kind of funny.

Has Santa ever met Jack Frost,
On a cold and wintery night?
Or the sandman met the tooth fairy
In my bedroom, what a sight!

I'm young and don't know everything,
But when I'm old I feel,
I'll have this mess all figured out,
And the magic will be real.

THE OLDEN DAYS

What was it like in the olden days,
Before color TV was here?
What did kids do to amuse themselves?
It really isn't clear.

No VCRs or rented tapes,
Or remotes to change the shows,
No video games, computers, or mice,
Or the joysticks to make them go.

I'm glad I'm young in the computer age,
Not like Mom and Dad, thank heaven,
Gosh, how'd they even learn to cook,
Without a microwave oven?

REFLECTIONS OF A PROMISE

A promise is a strange thing.
It's one of the strongest,
But most fragile things I know.
It's strength comes from
The trust behind it.
But it is fragile,
Because it is so easily broken.
I feel good when
I can rely on a promise
That is made to me.
But I feel cheated when
A promise made to me
Is broken.
So I must learn to choose
My promises carefully,
Because whether a promise
Is kept or broken,
It tells you nothing
About the promise itself,
But about the person who made it.

CHORES, CHORES, CHORES

Why am I the only one,
Who always has to work?
No one else does chores like me,
I feel like such a jerk.
Every day I must get dressed,
And then my bed I make,
I brush my teeth and pick up toys,
Please help, for heaven's sake!
And after school I clean my room,
My homework I must do,
Set the table, wash my hands,
I'm never, ever, through.
I cannot wait until I'm grown,
Won't do another chore,
I'll sit around and let my kids
Do them and much, much more.

SNACK

Well hi,
Mr. Fly.
Don't try
To fly
Into my...
(Gulp).
Oh my.
Good-bye!

TYING IS TRYING

Ever try to tie your shoe,
And make that darned old bow?
How'd they ever figure it out?
Beats me, I don't really know.

If you make short loops to have more lace,
The holes are way too small,
When you wind them around to pass them through,
The laces won't fit at all.

But if you make your loops quite big,
So the laces have room enough,
There's no lace left to make the bow,
I give up on all this stuff.

I've found the solution to all my woes,
Until I become a pro,
My Mom only buys me sneakers and shoes,
That stay closed with nice velcro!

HO......HUM

I'm bored.
There's nothing to do.
TV's boring.
Video games are boring.
My toys are boring.
The swings are boring.
Fighting is boring.
Life is boring.
Being bored is boring.
This poem is boring.

Has anyone ever died from boredom?

ABBREVS.

I'm glad I'm learning to read and write,
And I think I'm doing quite well,
But now and again I see these words,
That I can't seem to say or spell.

They're usually short, with very few vowels,
They don't make too much sense,
I'm told they're abbreviations,
And they make me feel very tense.

How do you read **Ltd**?
Or **Dr.** or **Ms.** or **Co**?
I cringe when I see **tpk.**,
Tell me it isn't so.

The days of the week get shortened,
From **Mon.** to **Sun.** you can't win,
The months aren't any better,
It's **Jan.** to **Dec.** and back again.

You must always be careful to watch
Your **mphs** when on the **hwy.**,
It's so exasperating,
I don't know what else to say.

Pkgs. aren't much better,
Their **net wt.** is **ozs.** and **lbs.**
And sometimes a **Co.** is really an **Inc.**,
How does all of this sound?

The states are a mess when you think of it,
Whether you live in **VT** or **CA**,
AZ, IA, WV, TX, MT, NJ,
None of these will get you far.

This problem is so bad, I think,
I might go on forever,
Like **Xmas** lines in the toy **dept.**,
Etc., etc., etc.....

CHICKEN POX

In the mirror,
I can see,
Little bumps,
All over me.

Look at them,
I'm one big blotch,
And, oh my gosh,
They itch a lot.

Bumps keep coming,
I hope it stops,
'Cause I don't like,
The chicken pox!

SHARING

How come I always have to share?
Why do they make me?
It just isn't fair.

Nobody wants to share your bad things,
They only want good
And whatever it brings.

Why can't I share the worst of my chores?
Or give away homework,
Or low bowling scores?

I guess people want all that is best,
But I don't want to share,
Just give it a rest!

RAINY DAY

What can you do
On a rainy day,
When you really can't go
Outside and play?

Use sofa cushions
In the den,
To make a fort
Covered with an afghan.

Get a big flashlight,
Hunt under the bed,
For long, lost treasures,
And get fuzzed, instead.

Make a tent with your covers
And fill it full,
Or wave them around
Like you're chasing a bull.

Make the laundry basket
A fancy car,
So your animals
Can go near and far.

There's so much stuff
To pretend about,
I never noticed
The sun came out.

APOLOGY

I'm sorry.
I didn't mean to do it....
Really.

It's okay.
I love you.

FOOD VACUUM

What's for breakfast?
What's for lunch?
I'm still hungry,
What can I munch?
When will we eat?
What's to drink?
Can I have a snack?
I'm starving, I think.
Three meals a day,
Just won't do,
I need to eat,
The whole day through!

CAN DREAMS COME TRUE?

Are dreams pretend,
Or are they real?
When I'm having them,
They're live, I feel.

Can they come true?
I just don't know,
But you always need dreams,
Wherever you go.

I cannot control
My dreams each night,
Or I'd get rid of those,
That give me a fright.

But I can choose,
Most definitely,
The dreams for my life,
What I want it to be.

And then I have
The choice, like you,
To work real hard,
And make them come true.

THINK BEFORE YOU SPEAK

Sometimes I wish that my words had strings,
So I could pull 'em back into my mouth,
I don't mean to say all those rotten things,
But somehow they jump right on out.

It seems like my mouth works much faster
Than my brain, which can't keep up the pace,
It stumbles, gets fresh, and some bad words come out,
They surprise me, just look at my face!

I better just try to control it,
Keep my mouth closed as much as can be,
But until I can get it to work right,
I hope that you'll please forgive me.

WHEN I GET OLD

What will I be like
When I get old?
My hair will be gray,
Maybe I'll be bald.
I'll probably move slow
Like a turtle or snail,
And everything will ache,
So I'll groan and wail.
I'll start to forget
Names and places and how,
And where I just put things,
It's no different now.
But the best thing of all,
It's so neat, don't you think?
I'll just take out my teeth,
And put 'em on the sink!

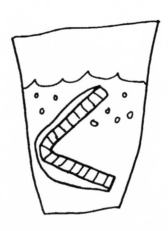

IT'S ALL RIGHT TO CRY

Sometimes,
When I'm angry, or hurt,
Or something makes me feel really bad,
The tears well up inside me,
And spill down my cheeks.
I try to hold them back,
But they come anyway.

And then I'm embarrassed.

But I think it's all right to cry,
Because when I'm done,
I feel a whole lot better.
And besides,
I've even seen my Dad do it.

LIFE GOES ON

It's neat to plant a seed in the spring,
And wait for it to sprout,
I guess I like to see it 'cause
It's what life is all about.

I plant and then I watch and wait,
Use water and some sun,
And when I see those heads poke up,
I squeal, it's so much fun.

When it gets too big for it's little pot,
In the house so safe and sound,
I take it out in the big, wide world,
And plant it in the ground.

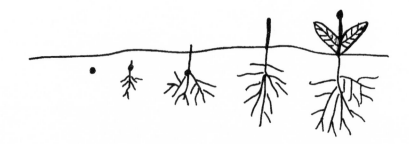

My plant grows big and flourishes,
I keep out all the weeds,
And then it finally gets a flower,
And makes new, tiny seeds.

I feel so proud, I really do,
The pleasure's beyond all worth,
I helped to make a pretty thing,
And beautify the earth.

And in the fall when it finally dies,
I want to shed a tear,
But then I realize it'll be all right,
When I start again next year.

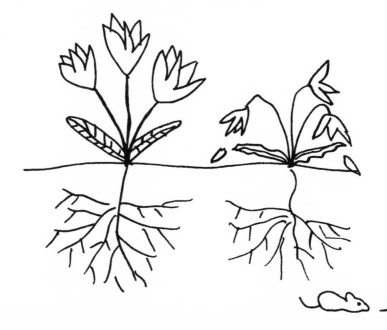

IF AT FIRST YOU DON'T SUCCEED....

They tell me I should never give up,
That I should always try,
But when I do and mess things up,
I always start to cry.

I feel so bad when a grownup does
Something so easily,
And then I try, but it's not the same,
I guess it must be me.

They're always right, and perfect, and sure,
And I'm just little and dumb,
I'll never do things as good as they can,
Why should I try, how come?

The only thing that I can think,
To help me stick it through,
Is that all these perfect, grownup people
Were little and dumb once, too!

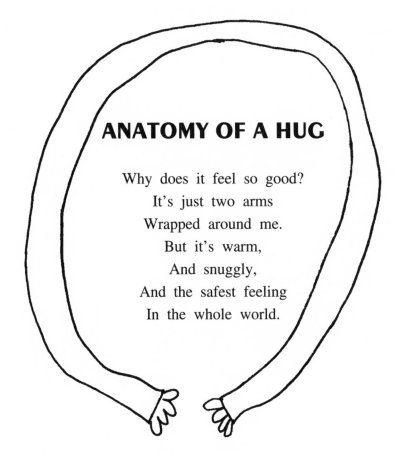

ANATOMY OF A HUG

Why does it feel so good?
It's just two arms
Wrapped around me.
But it's warm,
And snuggly,
And the safest feeling
In the whole world.

PASCHETTI ETIQUETTE

What's the best way to eat pasghetti?
I've got it all figured out,
Just shovel it in any old way,
You'll enjoy it, I have no doubt.

I've done this so long, I'm quite an expert,
So let me give you some tips,
If you suck the strands into your mouth,
All the sauce collects on your lips.

You can chop it all up into little bits,
But wait, don't do it too soon,
'Cause it takes away all the fun of it,
When you eat pasghetti with a spoon.

I like to twirl some around my fork,
And get a big clump to eat,
Then watch my mother's eyes bug out,
When I stuff my mouth, what a feat!

No matter how you get it in,
It always tastes so good,
And since it's so much fun to eat,
Pasghetti's my favorite food!

THE RULES ARE RIDICULOUS

How come the rules that apply to them,
Don't always apply to me?
Why can't I do all the things they do?
On this we never agree.

I'd like to drink soda whenever **I** want,
And stay up as late as can be,
Munch popcorn and pretzels and other junk food,
While I watch what **I** like on TV.

I'd never do anymore homework,
And I'd bathe just when **I** wanted to,
I'd stay up and have a big party,
Every night for the whole night through.

Then I'd sleep very late every morning,
And not worry 'bout going to school,
Things really would be so much better,
If **I** could make up all the rules!

LET'S GO FOR A DRIVE

Riding in the car is so much fun,
There's lots that you can do,
The only trouble with most of it,
Is the driver gets mad at you.

You can breathe on the windows and fog them up,
Fingerpaint and write your name,
Use an empty seat belt as a missile,
To me it's just a game.

I like to pretend I have a guitar,
With the long brush for the snow,
I sing and play my electric brush,
Along with the radio.

You can watch the cars along the road,
Feel the wind, how fast it can blow,
And when the driver isn't looking,
Launch some paper out the window.

I have so much fun when we go for a drive,
You can see as you read this poem,
I don't understand quite why it is,
My Mom would rather stay home.

WHAT DO I WANT TO BE
WHEN I GROW UP?

Someone who saves.

 Like a fireman, or doctor, or nurse.

Someone who protects.

 Like a policeman, or soldier, or lawyer.

Someone who leads.

 Like the President.

Someone who discovers and builds.

 Like a scientist or engineer.

Someone who guides.

 Like a teacher or minister.

Someone who creates beauty.

 Like an artist or writer.

Someone who does all of the above.

 Like Mom and Dad.

Someone who people can be proud of.

 Like me.

ODE TO AN ODE

What makes a poem a poem?
Does it always have to rhyme?
Hmmm....let me try to think this one out,
It may take a little time.

It's easy when all the words
Rhyme, and the verses fit,
But never forget that a poem,
Should have a point to it.

And sometimes
You have something
So powerful to say
That it flows
Like a waterfall,
But doesn't rhyme.
The beauty of it
Lies not only
In the message,
But in the pattern
Of the words
On the page.

So don't be afraid of poems,
They're a window into your soul,
Just put your feelings on paper,
And don't worry if you can't find the right word to finish.

PEST

Please scat,
Mr. Cat.
You're too fat,
And sat
On my hat.
Now it's flat.
Oh drat!

THE DUMB DICTIONARY

The dictionary is a useless book,
It makes me very mad,
In order to use the darned old thing,
You need to be prepared.

You want to use it if you can't spell
A word you really need,
But you need to know how to spell the word,
To look it up, indeed!

Have you ever heard of such a thing?
I surely never did,
It doesn't even have good words,
Like **rediculus** and **stoopid.**

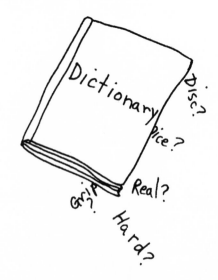

NOW YOU SEE IT
NOW YOU DON'T

Can't see wind,
But I know it's here,
All around us,
It's the air.
Can't see music,
But I know it's here,
Listen to it,
With my ear.
Can't see love,
But I know it's here,
My heart can feel it,
Everywhere.

THE LAST WORD

Did not.
Did to.

Did not!
Did to!

DID NOT!
DID TO!

DID NOT!
DID TO!

STOP IT!

Okay.
Okay.

Did not....

GIGGLEPUSS

Once you start 'em, you can't stop 'em,
They take hold and won't let go,
Doesn't matter if it's funny,
Giggles seem to grow and grow.

The more you try, the worse it gets,
The giggles just increase,
They make you act so dumb and silly,
They never want to cease.

I always seem to get in trouble,
When I get a giggle attack,
But when it's over, I'll tell you a secret,
I can't wait for them to come back!

BEAUTY IS IN THE EYE
OF THE BEHOLDER

My favoritest flower in the whole wide world,
Is one that you can rely on,
Each spring it comes so bright and strong,
The mighty Dandy Lion.

A bright yellow army springs forth with pride,
As quickly as can be,
This sea of yellow in a dull green lawn,
Is a pretty sight to me.

I pick whole bunches to give away,
To my teacher and Mom and friends,
And there's still more left when I am done,
They never seem to end.

Then a funny change begins to take place,
Like caterpillars, I guess,
The flowers become like butterflies,
All graceful fluffiness.

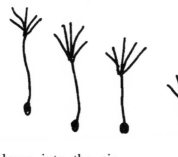

Puffy fireworks blown into the air,
They scatter without a sound,
The flower is naked and no more fun,
But there's more to blow around.

No other flower gives so much pleasure,
And always returns so strong,
The Dandy Lion doesn't need any care,
As it spreads throughout your lawn.

Most people don't like the Dandy Lion,
They kill it wherever it shows,
But since it's such a wonderful flower,
Why's it a weed?   Who knows?

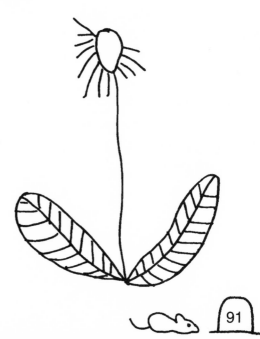

THE MOST POWERFUL THING

Which has more power -
Your heart or your brain?

Must be your heart.
Your heart keeps your body alive.
But if your heart is beating and your brain is dead -
Do you have any life?

Must be your brain.
Your brain controls every part of your body.
But your heart controls your feelings
Which can control you.

Must be your heart.
Your heart makes you feel really bad sometimes.
But your brain can do really bad things too,
Like give you nightmares.

Must be your brain.
Your brain can take you places you've never been.
But your heart can give you love,
The most powerful thing in the world.

Must be your heart.

STUBBORN

I don't want to,
I don't care,
I won't do it,
I'm not scared.

You can't make me,
Just you try,
If you hit me,
I'll make you cry.

Give it up,
I won't give in,
Nah, nah, nah, nah, nah,
Nah, nah, nah..........thbbbt!.

EVERYTHING
IN MODERATION

Everything in moderation,
Not too much of this or that,
Got to keep your life in balance,
Or get in trouble, it's a fact.

Too much work will stress you out,
And too much play is wrong,
Too much food will make you fat,
How can you ever live long?

Too much worry will make you sick,
And too much time is lonely,
Too much liquor will make you drunk,
I'll tell you this once only:

There are just two things you need in extremes,
To live to a hundred and one,
They're laughter and an attitude
That looks at life as fun!

BATHTUB NAVY

A-floating in the tub,
A-way, way, out at sea,
All my ships and ducks and men,
Are ready to save me.

Torpedoed by the soap,
And capsized by a wave,
I'll have to check the damage,
And see what I can save.

A washcloth bomb gets dropped
In the middle of my fleet,
Plastic bodies all around,
Collecting at my feet.

The monsoons are a-coming,
The faucet makes it rain,
The plug is pulled, the whirlpool starts,
They're headed down the drain!

I save them with my toes,
I wish I had more power,
What will happen to my fleet,
When I learn to take a shower?

DINNER MAP

Mashed potato mountains
And a gravy moat,
Meatloaf slice meadows
And a butter bread boat.

A creamed spinach swamp
Held back by a spoon,
Where to put my carrot swords?
There's no more room.

My map keeps changing shape,
It's looking rather funny,
A few more bites and then
It'll wind up in my tummy!

WHO'S RESPONSIBLE
FOR RESPONSIBILITY?

I'm doing the best I can.
But the more I do,
The more they want me to do.

They call it responsibility.

That means:
Act your age.
Do what you're told to do.
Show that you can be trusted.

I don't want responsibility.

They don't like it when I act my age.
I never get to tell anyone else what to do.
No one ever trusts me enough
To give me a chance to be trusted.

So what's the answer?

Maybe grownups should be
More responsible,
When teaching kids to be
More responsible.

IT'S TOO HARD
TO BE
A SOURPUSS

When I get mad I try my best,
To pout and sulk and frown,
But then I remember a frown is just
A smile upside down.

The harder I try to frown and grump,
And keep a sour face,
The quicker the edges of my lips,
Curl up with a smile in place.

You can't really frown for very long,
A smile will always win,
It's stronger, and besides it's normal,
For your mouth to want to grin.

FLIGHT OF FANCY

I can pump so hard that I
Can make my swing go up so high
That I can almost kick the sky.

It's nice for me to feel so free,
Flying higher than the trees,
The wind keeps pushing, tickling me.

The more I pump the higher I go,
My heart beats faster, then I know,
The excitement's why I love it so.

Maybe if I pump real fast,
My swing will then take off at last,
I'll watch the world go rushing past.

I'll glide along just like a bird,
Touch mountains, clouds, and all I've heard.
Life from above, more beautiful than words.

I'd like to soar, to go away,
But attached to earth I guess I'll stay,
Perhaps I'll fly somehow, someday.

So when I want to slow it down,
I drag my feet upon the ground,
My flight is over without a sound.

TEENY TINY MESS

Why do they always
Get so upset?
It's just a
       teeny,
        tiny
        mess.

Clothes scattered around,
From when I got dressed,
It's just a
       teeny,
        tiny
        mess.

Damp towels on the floor,
A swamp at its best,
It's just a
       teeny,
        tiny
        mess.

A rumpled bed,
I'm not out to impress,
It's just a
       teeny,
        tiny
        mess.

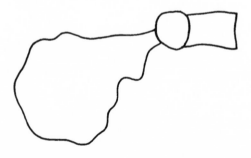

Some milk on the table,
Causes distress?
It's just a
       teeny,
        tiny
       mess.

Bikes in the street,
I couldn't care less,
It's just a
       teeny,
        tiny
       mess.

A few toys on the ground,
I left them, I guess,
It's just a
       teeny,
        tiny
       mess.

Put all together,
I must confess,
They make one

BIG,
GIGANTIC
MESS!

PERMISSION

I'm supposed to ask
Before I take,
Or go, or do,
Don't make mistakes.

Can't eat cookies
At 5 o'clock,
Or ride my bike
Around the block.

Can't cross the street
All by myself,
Or get a plate
From the highest shelf.

Can't bring sticks
Into the house,
Or rocks, or worms,
Or even a mouse.

Can't stick clay
In all my toys,
Or run inside
And make lots of noise.

This permission stuff
Is pretty dumb,
It certainly makes
My life no fun.

COCOON

A place to play,
To think,
To snuggle in.
I go there when
I'm scared.
Or mad.
Or tired.
Safe from all.
It beckons me.
My bed.

THE DENTIST PARADOX

Dentists are such funny folk,
Who have a funny quirk,
They try the hardest that they can,
To put themselves out of work.

They teach you how to brush and floss,
And take good care of your mouth,
But what would they do with nothing to fix?
Close up shop and go south?

They're very sad when your teeth aren't well,
And your gums are red and throb,
But if we all had perfect teeth,
Dentists would be out of a job.

And so I'll try to do my part,
Even if it's just a cleaning,
I have to do a few things wrong,
To give my dentist's life meaning.

MY GRAND PARENTS

Grams and Gramps, Nana and Pop,
They've all got special names,
Grandmas and Grandpas get called different things,
I love 'em just the same.

They're not like Mom and Dad, you know,
They give me lots of treats,
And then say, *"Shhh, don't tell your Mom,"*
I think they're really neat.

I always win, no matter what
The game is that we play,
I try to help them, but I guess
They're old, what can I say?

My Grandma always cooks the best,
And makes whatever I choose,
She always lets me have dessert,
It's great, how can I lose?

My Grandpa likes to take me out,
Catch up on news, you see,
I think I love them both because
They always have time for me.

They're tired now, I understand,
And not in the mood for jokes,
'Cause instead of a kid like me to raise,
They had to put up with my folks!

BUBBLE GUM

How can something so little,
Be so much fun?
And taste so good?
Mmmm....bubble gum.
Is it a food?
Or is it a toy?
You can't really eat it,
But it gives lots of joy.
Humongous bubbles,
I make 'em pop,
When I start chewing gum,
I can never stop.
Half the wad from my mouth,
Makes strings that hang long,
I'll only stop chewing,
When the flavor's all gone.
So if you're real bored,
With no room to play,
Get some bubble gum,
To brighten your day!

FORGIVENESS

Is it harder
To apologize or to forgive?
I'm not sure.
If you apologize,
You're admitting you were wrong.
And that hurts your pride.
If you forgive,
You're saying you understand,
That it's all right anyway.
And that hurts your sense of fairness.
But the answer doesn't matter,
Because you can't forgive someone
Unless they are willing
To apologize first....

Or can you?

IT'S MY LEFT, RIGHT?

Left is thisaway, right is thataway,
I get myself confused,
Just when I think I have it straight,
I have to put on my shoes.

Go to the left, and go to the right,
It seems like such a maze,
But I remember Mom taught me
To sort it out two ways:

Hold your fists up in the air,
With pointers up and thumbs straight out,
The one that makes a forward "L,"
Is your left hand, I've no doubt.

The other way is easy, too,
To tell both directions apart,
All I have to remember is,
My left side's the one with my heart.

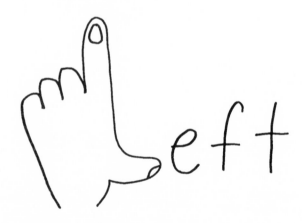

I, ME, GIMME

I want it....
But you didn't get me....
I want this one, too....
I don't like it....
Can I have?....
Where's mine?....
I didn't want *that*....
But you got *him* one....

We come into the world with nothing.
We leave the world with nothing.
Why do we spend our whole lives wanting everything?

EARS THE PROBLEM

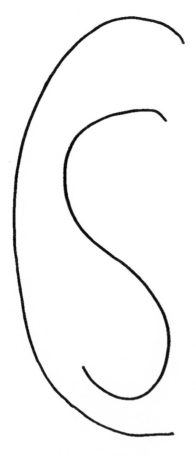

Ears are such
A funny thing,
Why do we have them?
I'm wondering.

Some are big,
And some are small,
Some stick way out,
Some don't at all.

They look silly,
From near or far,
Like doors left open
On a waiting car.

In a drawing,
They seem out of place,
Two parentheses
Stuck on a face.

Without ears

We might look good,
But how'd we hear?
I doubt we could.

We'd try to use
Something else, I suppose,
Like trying to hear
Right through our nose.

This poem is goofy,
They're here to stay,
I'll keep my ears,
Now....what'd you say?

SECRET WEAPON

I can get my Mom so mad,
She certainly pays attention,
It's really so easy that it is
Too obvious to mention.
I always have it with me,
This ultimate weapon of mine,
When Mom refuses to listen to me,
I let out a great, big whine.

SODA ODE

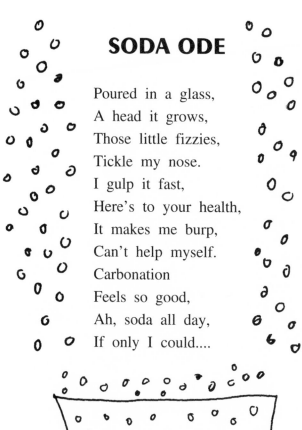

Poured in a glass,
A head it grows,
Those little fizzies,
Tickle my nose.
I gulp it fast,
Here's to your health,
It makes me burp,
Can't help myself.
Carbonation
Feels so good,
Ah, soda all day,
If only I could....

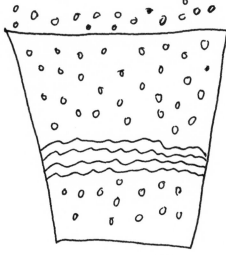

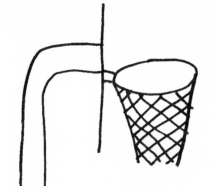

WHERE DO I BELONG?

I want to be a part of the group,
I want so much to fit in,
I want them to want to be with me,
I'll just wait here until then.

I want to be so popular,
I want to be picked first,
I want to share in the things they do,
Can the waiting be any worse?

They never seem to seek me out,
Or include me in all the fun,
Why can't I ever be one of them?
It makes me want to run.

It's lonely here, I want to cry,
But still I have my pride,
Why does this always happen to me?
I need to look inside.

Perhaps I'm not really like all of them,
And maybe that isn't so bad,
I know I can get through life on my own,
I have strength, and that makes me glad.

The hurt's still there, it'll always be
A reminder that I can't ignore,
But I'll use it to make my life more worthwhile,
Of this I can be sure.

For I know what it's like to be left out,
To be by myself in the end,
So when I see a kid all alone,
I'll try to be his friend.

FIRST ONE UP IN THE MORNING

All silent,
Except for the birds.
Cool breezes
Flap at the shade.
The smells are sweet
From an outdoors wet with dew.
Dawn peeks through the window....

A new day.

STICKY PREDICAMENT

What's new?
Mr. Shoe?
Quite a few
Say that you
Stepped in glue.
Now you're blue,
And stuck, too,
Is it true?
What'll you do?
I haven't a clue.
Boo-hoo.

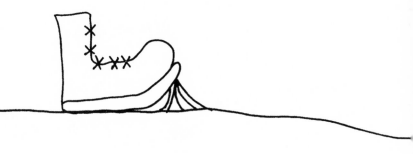

IS LIFE JUST A MEMORY?

Some people live in the past.
Is it because they are unhappy
With their lives now?
Do their memories comfort them
And protect them from everyday?

Some people want to forget their pasts.
They live only for today
And what is yet to come.
Is it because their memories
Are too painful to recall?

Some people are in between.
They remember some and forget some.
Are their lives in balance?
Do the good and bad memories
Help them make decisions now?

It seems like no matter what,
Our lives today are shaped
By all that went on before.

GARBAGE TRUCK

Rumble, rumble, SQUEAL!
Crash, bang, boom,
Rumble, rumble, **SQUEAL!**
Rev, rev, vrooom.

Crash, bang, boom,
For heaven's sake,
Rumble, rumble, ***SQUEAL!!***
FIX THOSE BRAKES!

THE MOUNTAIN
OF LAUNDRY

It's always there,
It's all around,
Baskets of laundry,
It's on the ground.

Empty drawers,
No clothes to wear,
Out of laundry,
It isn't fair.

Hamper's stuffed,
It's in the way,
Here's some more,
To put away.

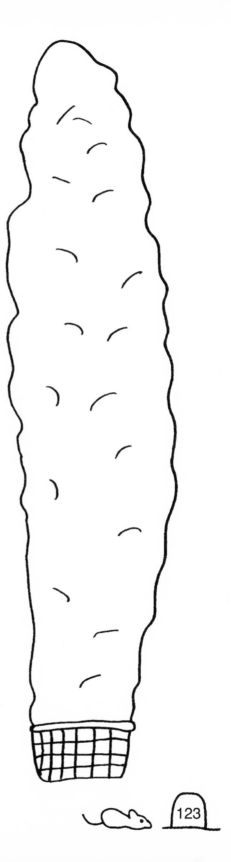

Baskets of clothes,
So clean and sweet,
Need to be sorted,
And folded so neat.

I don't understand
Why it's always there,
The mountain of laundry
Will never disappear.

Well, all this work
Has made me sweat,
Let me change my clothes,
We're not done yet!

A FACT OF LIFE

No matter how much
Other people care,
The only one
Who can do something
About me
Is me.

THE SUPER MARKET

I love to go to the grocery store,
It's loads and loads of fun,
You get to see what you saw on TV,
And try to get Mom to buy some.

There's snacks and gum and crackers and nuts,
Yummy cookies and all sorts of stuff,
The cereals are the bestest of all,
I never can get quite enough.

There's pizza and chips and ice cream delights,
And the sweetest drinks that you can find,
The donuts and cakes seem to leap out at me,
It drives me right out of my mind.

There's only one thing I can't understand,
Since my Mom knows I love it so,
Why does she shop when I'm stuck in school?
Why won't she let me go?

PAIN

When I have it,
I can't think
Of anything else.
It makes me want
To scream,
Or cry.
Sometimes I can use
A bandage for it.
But the hardest pain of all
To make better,
Is the pain
In my heart.

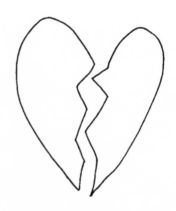

LITTLE WHITE LIE

I do not understand why she,
Will never, ever believe me.
The stories that I tell are true,
This I gladly swear to you.
Maybe I might slightly embellish,
'Cause I'm afraid I might get punished.
A little fact, just one or two,
But darn, she always can see through.
I wonder how it is that she,
Always, always catches me.
Can't she see I really try?
I would never, ever lie.

BUGGY

Oh, gee,
Mr. Flea.
I can't see
You on me.
Heed my plea,
And feel free,
To leave me.
So can we
Both agree
This can't be?
(Scratch, scratch)....
Tee-hee.

OPPOSITES

Break, fix,
Always, never,
All, none,
Apart, together.

Push, pull,
Give, take,
Hurt, cure,
Asleep, awake.

Hate, love,
Past, future,
Worse, better,
Certain, unsure.

Some opposites really aren't that far apart.

TRAFFIC

Why aren't we moving?
Why's it so slow?
Can't you step on it?
Why don't we go?
Where'd these cars come from?
Where are they going?
Why's that truck moving past?
What is it towing?
Why's that car steaming?
Why'd it overheat?
When will we get there?
What'da we have to eat?
Why's that car racing by?
Why don't we try it?
Can't we drive on the grass?
What d'ya mean, be quiet?

WHAT'S FAIR IS FAIR

Hers is bigger.
I want my share.
They're not even.
It's not fair.

I didn't do it.
Don't you care?
Why punish me?
It's not fair.

Me clean up?
How can you dare?
They made this mess.
It's not fair.

Just to be in charge,
I'd say a prayer,
Then decide for grownups,
It's only fair.

LECTRICITY

It goes through the wall so very fast,
And spills out from an outlet,
I'm talkin' 'bout lectricity,
Most dangerous thing I've met.

It's powerful, does lots of good,
And handles better than fire,
Runs toasters, vacuums, microwaves,
All from a little wire.

You can't see it, but it's there,
It's tempting, like a drug,
But listen to me, tried it once,
Don't ever play with a plug.

If you stick it in the outlet,
With fingers touching a prong,
You'll get a shock that's big enough,
To remember for very long.

Lectricity runs through your body,
Until it reaches the ground,
Not only does it scare you bad,
It hurts you all around.

I like to play with lots of things,
Like you do, I suspect,
But stay away from lectricity,
And treat it with respect.

UPHILL ALL THE WAY

Everything is a struggle.
Nothing's ever easy.
Why can't something
Just go right for once?
That's life, I guess.

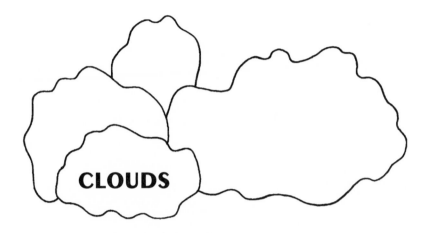

CLOUDS

Marshmallow fluff up in the sky,
Cotton candy floating high,
Softly drifting,
Warm, uplifting,
Clouds keep passing by.

When I am in a certain mood,
Nothing makes me feel as good,
They do their part,
As flying art,
I'd touch them if I could.

Sometimes the shapes that clouds can be,
Are pictures or a mystery,
Sunsets perfected,
All colors reflected,
Clouds are beauty to me.

SPIDER SURPRISE

You find them in the strangest places,
Behind the doors and under the bed,
In the corners around the room,
They're something that I dread.

Dangling from the ceiling,
Like a tiny trapeze act,
The spider quickly spins its line,
No time to think, just react.

They always seem to sneak on up,
Wherever I happen to be,
I want someone to come squish them,
But then I think, oh gee....

The spider is a good bug,
He's not really in my way,
But why does he have to surprise me?
It nearly ruins my day.

So spiders, it would help you,
To live longer lives, I hope,
If you made some noise or something,
And didn't scare the wits out of folks!

BODY LANGUAGE

Ah-choo!....Bless you.

       Thanks, you know.

Yawn....You tired?

       Nah, let's go.

Cough....Cover your mouth.

       I won't forget.

Hiccup....BOO!

       They're not gone yet.

Blush....You embarrassed?

       No, not really.

BURRRP!....Who did that?

       Oh, excuse me.

THE SKY'S THE LIMIT

A long, long time ago,
Man looked up at the stars
And said, "I want to be there."
> *And everyone laughed.*
> *But he had a dream.*

So he studied and studied,
And learned everything
That he could.
> *And everyone laughed.*
> *But he became educated.*

He tried and tried, but he couldn't make it.
Each time he tried,
He got a little bit better.
> *And everyone laughed.*
> *But he learned from his mistakes.*

Then he found he couldn't do it alone.
He found people to help him,
People to share his dream.
> *And everyone laughed.*
> *But he cooperated.*

It was scary out there,
But he was determined to face it,
To make it work.

> *And everyone laughed.*
> *But he had courage.*

Many, many years passed,
And he still didn't realize his dream.
It didn't seem possible.

> *And everyone laughed.*
> *But he didn't give up.*

Now, if you look up at the stars,
We're there.
Man's dream came true.

> *And no one is laughing.*
> *Everyone is proud.*

The only limits we have
Are the ones we place
On ourselves.

> *So don't laugh.*
> *Get yourself a dream.*

JUST A WHISTLIN' FOOL

Pucker up
And blow some air through,
Can't you whistle?
Don't know how to?
It's so easy,
Watch my lips,
Then I'll give you
My secret tips.
Blow real gentle,
Lips real tight,
Move your tongue
Around just right.
Easy now,
And take it slow,
It took me days
To learn, you know.
When you're an expert,
In a while,
You'll learn to whistle
As you smile.

ALMOST
EVERYTHING IS RELATIVE

When you can't do it, before you learn how,
Gosh, everything's hard at first,
But then you learn and it's a cinch,
It definitely could be worse.

Things that were bigger are now much smaller,
Seems most things shrink with time,
The jungle gym that scared you once,
You now can easily climb.

Some kids in school are smarter than you,
And some are certainly not,
Some friends you'll find have less than you,
And others have more than you've got.

The thing to remember throughout your life,
Whether you win or fail,
Is time eventually evens things out,
But justice won't always prevail.

You need to look inside of yourself,
Find whatever you like the best,
Then make the most of those things that you can,
And forget about all the rest.

UH OH....

Tantrums come up very sneaky,
Get you riled and oh so mad,
Don't they know I never mean it?
Hope they don't think that I'm bad.

Most days I am calm and nice,
But sometimes when I slip,
I get myself so angry that
I lose control and let 'er rip.

It takes a lot to get me going,
I don't have big screaming fits,
After all, I'm bigger now,
And tantrums are for little kids.

I can handle anything,
But there's one thing that strikes a blow,
It's when they think I'm having a tantrum,
And I know it just ain't so.

I mean, that's nerve -
Me, a tantrum? Never!
I'm big now.
I'm ALWAYS calm.
Why do you say I'm having a tantrum?
It's YOU that has the problem!
NOT **ME**!!
CALM DOWN??!!
STOP TELLING ME WHAT TO DO!!!!
I AM *NOT* YELLING!!!!!

THE ICING ON THE CAKE

Beaters, beaters, love them beaters,
Please leave lots of frosting on,
If you bang them on the bowl edge,
All the good stuff will be gone.

It's a challenge just to lick 'em,
Twist my tongue through every hole,
When I'm finished with the beaters,
Will you let me clean the bowl?

Decorations, oh so pretty,
What a creation you can make,
As for me, I'll take the frosting,
You can have the rest of the cake!

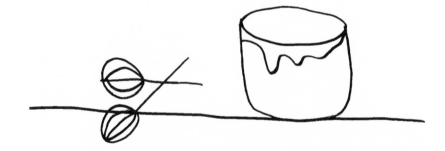

ODE TO NOISE

Whistles, sirens,
Shrieks and yells,
Motorcycles,
Loud church bells.
Screaming kids,
A slamming door,
Big lawn mowers,
And much more.
Blasting radios,
A fire truck,
Squealing tires,
A car horn that's stuck.
These sounds are great,
Please don't think small,
The louder, the better,
I love 'em all.
The only sound
That makes no sense,
Is perfect, complete
Dead silence.

DUST IN THE AIR

Dust in the air,
Dust in the air,
I love to watch
The dust in the air.
It swirls all around,
In the bright morning sun,
And sparkles a lot,
It's really such fun!
They dance and they bump,
And float to the ground,
Those dust molecules
Are all around.
But they're very shy,
Don't like to play,
When a cloud comes by,
They go away!

A QUESTION OF TIME

How long is forever?
Will you be here then?
How long do we live?
Will the world ever end?

Don't worry about it.
Our lives are long,
But forever is longer.
Just make the most
Of the time that you have.

TAIL TALE

Wouldn't it be fun
To have a nice tail?
They're useful and pretty,
And don't ever fail.

If you were a dog,
You could wag it all day,
To show you were happy,
And wanted to play.

If you were a cow,
You could swish at your sides,
To keep yourself cool,
And brush away flies.

If you were a cat,
You could lie in one place,
Then your tail warmly wrap,
Around your soft face.

If you were a fish,
And wanted to swim,
You'd just move your tail,
And slap with your fins.

If your were a kangaroo,
And wanted to rest,
You could lean on your tail,
A chair at its best.

If you were a possum,
With a tail so strong,
You could hang upside down,
And sleep all day long.

But for me, well, I guess,
I'll make do with my hands,
For alas, a long tail,
Won't fit in my pants!

THE POWER OF LIGHT

When you open the door
To a dark room,
And there is light outside,
It pushes its way into the darkness.

But when you open the door
To a lighted room,
And there is darkness outside,
It never comes in.

The same is true
For your heart and mind.

PLACE YOUR POEM
HERE

PLACE YOUR POEM
HERE

ACKNOWLEDGEMENTS

First and foremost, I'd like to thank God for making this creation come to life (not just me, but this book also). He has enabled me to write and given me the strength and perseverance to bring this project to fruition. My purpose has been to validate our human frailties and to share His message of hope and unconditional love and forgiveness with as many people as possible.

It is obvious that I must also thank the four most wonderful people in my life - my husband, Doug, and my three sons for their unwavering love and support. This project became a thread throughout our lives for several years. It took on a life of its own and without their talents as subject matter, illustrators, critics, and editors this book would not exist today.

Next, I would like to thank all of my relatives and very good friends who never gave up on this project - you know who you are, and there are too many to mention here. This includes all of the children and teachers to whom I've read. Your collective belief in the value of this work kept me going in the face of relentless and unceasing rejection.

And finally, more specifically, many thanks to Pam Shapiro for lending her artistic eye and suggestions regarding page layout and cover design.

Thank you all - we **FINALLY** did it!

Diane

INDEX

To order additional copies of **THE GIANT AND THE MOUSE:**

a.) I want to order _____ books @ $ 9.95 per book   = $ _____

b.) NJ residents add 6% sales tax   = $ _____

c.) Add $2.00 shipping and handling for the first book

     and $ .50 for each additional book   = $ _____

Enclosed please find my check or money order (no cash or CODs) payable to Hereami Publishing, in the amount of (total lines a. b. & c.) $ _____.

The books should be shipped to:

        Name _____

        Address _____

        City _____ State _____ Zip _____

Mail this order form and your check or money order to (allow 4-6 weeks for delivery):
      Hereami Publishing, P.O. Box 261 Butler, NJ 07405-0261
If you have any questions, please call (201) 838-2685 or fax (201) 492-1525.

To order additional copies of **THE GIANT AND THE MOUSE:**

a.) I want to order _____ books @ $ 9.95 per book   = $ _____

b.) NJ residents add 6% sales tax   = $ _____

c.) Add $2.00 shipping and handling for the first book

     and $ .50 for each additional book   = $ _____

Enclosed please find my check or money order (no cash or CODs) payable to Hereami Publishing, in the amount of (total lines a. b. & c.) $ _____.

The books should be shipped to:

        Name _____

        Address _____

        City _____ State _____ Zip _____

Mail this order form and your check or money order to (allow 4-6 weeks for delivery):
      Hereami Publishing, P.O. Box 261 Butler, NJ 07405-0261
If you have any questions, please call (201) 838-2685 or fax (201) 492-1525.